中 国 风 筝
Chinese Kites

U0133173

外文出版社

Foreign Languages Press

Written and Compiled by: Liu Chungen
Design by:
Photographs by: Liu Chungen, Sun Shuming,
Wang Wentong, Qu Weibo,
Dong Ruichen and Teng Shaowen
Cover design by: Tang Shaowen
Edited by: Liu Chungen

First Edition 2001

Chinese Kites

ISBN 7-119-02669-0

©Foreign Languages Press
Published by Foreign Languages Press
24 Baiwanzhuang Road, Beijing 100037, China
Home Page: http://www.flp.com.cn
E-mail Addresses: info@flp.com.cn
sales@flp.com.cn
Printed in the People's Republic of China

前　言

　　湛蓝的天空中，一只只风筝在飘荡、盘旋、翻飞，如鱼龙遨游在云水间，鹰、雁翱翔于长空，仙者驾云飞升……更有些风筝上附有音响装置，传出隐隐约约的声音，像是天外仙乐。中国风筝艺术给予人的美感，既有艺术品造型美、绘画的形象美，又有舞蹈般的动感美和音乐的听觉美，以及与自然环境相结合的意境美。众美归之，难怪几千年来，奇巧新颖的游戏方式层出不穷，人们却始终对扎制、放飞风筝乐而不倦。

　　中国是风筝的故乡。风筝发明已有两千五百多年的历史。据《韩非子·外储说左上》记载"墨子（约公元前468－前316年）斫木为鹞，三年而成，"飞一日而败"。也有的学者认为风筝起源还要早些。风筝是随舟船航行开始后而发明的。考古发现证实中国人在商殷时期（约公元前17世纪－约公元前11世纪），就掌握了航海技术。

　　风筝在中国诞生后，逐渐地传到了世界各地。英国学者李约瑟博士著的《中国科技史》中说，公元12世纪中国风筝传入欧洲，他认为这是中华民族向欧洲传播的重大科学发明之一。风筝传入日本要早一些。日本学者普遍认为风筝是在中国唐代（公元618-907年）时由日本遣唐使，从中国带回到日本的，后传至东南亚等地。

　　中国风筝最早是用竹木制作，名为"木鸢"，后来用丝绸制作的风筝叫"凤巾"，再后用纸张制作的风筝叫"纸鸢"。中国地域广阔，风筝的名称也有所不同，如叫"纸鸢"、"木鸢""凤鸢"、"鹞子"、"风瓦"等等。

　　"风筝"一名，据记载最早出现于宋代（公元960-1279年），宋高承著《事物纪原》中。据记载五代后汉（公元947-950）时的大臣李邺在纸鸢上安放了一种类似竹笛发音的装置，放飞时"使风入竹，如鸣筝"。人们把这种纸鸢叫"风筝"。后来也就把能放上天的各种"鸢"，统叫"风筝"。

　　17世纪后是中国风筝发展的鼎盛时期，这时的风筝无论在样式、扎制技术、装饰绘画及放飞技巧上均比过去有了很大的进步。到了近代，放风筝已成为全国范围内的群众娱乐活动，风筝制法上也出现了新构思、新技术和新材料。各地出现了不少的风筝流派。

　　风筝在中国的北方主要产于北京、天津、山东等地，南方为江苏、浙江一带。

风筝的画面图案多选取寓意吉祥的花、鸟、虫、兽组成，如象征富贵的牡丹，报春的燕子，与"福"字谐音的蝙蝠，喻意长寿的"猫、蝶"等。人形风筝所绘的人物形象多出自中国古典文学作品和神话传说，且是民间喜闻乐见的人物形象。如神怪小说《西游记》中的唐僧及其三位亦神亦人的徒弟：孙悟空、猪八戒、沙和尚；广行善事的道家"八仙"；以自酿的美酒为西王母祝寿的仙女麻姑……

风筝在历史发展的进程中，起过重要的作用。现代的航天器的雏形是风筝，恐怕无人怀疑。美国华盛顿史密斯宇航博物馆内，有一块说明牌上就写着"人类最早的飞行器是中国的风筝和火箭。"中国的一些史料中也多处记录了古代中国人利用风筝载人和测量高度及距离。同时也将风筝用于军事，风筝不但能测出敌军的距离，而且还能往外输送消息及物质。

风筝传到国外后，世界各国人民对风筝的运用就更广泛了。1804 年美国人制作了很像风筝的飞行器。1826 年英国人发明了用风筝作动力牵引的"飞车"。1874 年美国一无名者利用风筝渡过 240 米宽的峡谷。19 世纪法国人利用风筝成功地进行了一次海难救助。这些都是飞机发明前，人们经常利用的飞行器。

西方一些著名的科学家也曾利用风筝进行过许多重要的科学实验。苏格兰的威尔松在 1749 年把温度计绑在六个串联起来的风筝上，然后放飞到天空，再慢慢地让其降下，以测定不同高度的温度。1752 年美国科学家富兰克林在闪电时把系有金属丝的风筝放上天，揭开了雷电的秘密，证明空中闪电和电机发出的电是同一种"电物质"。英国气象学家在 1833 年利用风筝测量风速，取得了一系列数据。从此，风筝开始正式作为气象工具而被使用。20 世纪初，科学家科罗埃蒙·马可尼利用风筝作天线，与塞德·琼斯在大西洋两岸进行了无线电信号传送试验，获得了成功。

总之在过去一系列的科学试验中，风筝发挥了不可取代的作用。在今后的科学技术发展和未来的生活中风筝肯定还会发挥更大的作用。

放风筝不仅可以自娱、娱人，好的风筝还是馈赠亲朋好友的珍贵礼品，也可陈列于家中供欣赏和装饰环境。

自从风筝产生后，它就逐渐成为我国各民族人民喜欢的一项娱乐活动，由于各地的民俗民情及群众审美观念的不同，各地风筝在扎制、造型、装饰、绘画及放飞的技巧上，都形成了各自的地方特色。为了宏扬发展风筝艺术，中国各地的风筝协会经常举行风筝比赛、交流风筝发展中的经验。现在世界很多国家都有风筝协会，各国互相邀请国外的风筝爱好者参加比赛，交流扎制风筝的心得体会。

中国山东省潍坊市的风筝节就是一项在国内外比较有影响的风筝比赛。它不但促进了中国风筝艺术及世界风筝艺术的发展，也增进了各国人民的友谊，同时为潍坊的经济、旅游事业的发展起了重要的推动作用。

《韩非子·外储说左上》记载墨子是中国风筝最早的制造者
It is recorded in the book *Han Fei Zi* that Mo Zi was the earliest maker of kites in China.

1987年吉林省怀代县出土金代（公元1115－1234年）铸有放风筝的铜镜
A bronze mirror of the Kin dynasty (115-1234) cast with a picture of kite flying was unearthed at Huaidai County, Jilin Province in 1987.

Foreword

When kites fly, float and wheel in a clear blue sky, they are like fish and dragons swimming in water, eagles and swan geese gliding through the air and celestials riding on clouds. There are kites equipped with musical devices which emit sound like music from space. Many of the Chinese kites are works of art. Because of their beautiful shapes, the beautiful pictures painted on them, their rhythmic movements, the pleasant music they produce and their harmonious merging with natural surroundings, people have continued to introduce new gadgets to the kite and never lost interest in making and flying kites in the past several thousand years.

China is the birthplace of kites with a history of more than 2,500 years. According to the book *Han Fei Zi* , "Mo Zi [c.468-316 B.C.] cut wood to make a kite and completed it in three years. It flew for a whole day before it came down." Some scholars believe kites originated long before that time and was invented by sailors on their seafaring trips. Archaeological finds prove that navigation skills were mastered by the Chinese in the Shang-Yin time in the 17th-11th centuries B.C.

After their birth in China, kites gradually found their way to other parts of the world. In his book *Science and Civilization in China*, Dr. J. Needham said that kites were brought to Europe in the 12th century. He believed that kites were one of the important Chinese scientific inventions introduced to Europe. Kites were taken to Japan at a still earlier date. Japanese scholars generally believe that they were brought to Japan by Japanese envoys to the court of the Tang dynasty (618-907). Later, kites also found their way to places in Southeast Asia.

The earliest Chinese kites were made with bamboo and wood and were called "wooden kites." When kites were made with silk and satin later, they were called "wind scarf." Still later, when kites were covered with paper, they were called "paper kites." As China is extensive in area, kites were called by different names in different places, such as paper, wooden and wind kites, hawks or wind tiles. "Fengzheng" (wind zithers) the Chinese name for kites, first appeared in written record during the Song dynasty (960-1279). The book *Records of the Origin of Things* written by Gao Cheng of the Song dynasty states that during the Later Han dynasty (947-950) of the Five Dynasties period, a senior official named Li Ye attached a bamboo pipe to a kite. "When wind blew into the pipe, it produced a sound like that of a zither." People then began to call this kind of kites "wind zithers," a name which later applied on all types of kites.

After the 17th century, kites in China went through a period of brilliant development. Great progress was made in the styles of the kites, the skills of making them, the decorations and pictures painted on them and the skill of flying them. During the modern period, kite flying has become a nationwide popular pastime. New ideas, skills and materials were introduced into the making of kites. There have appeared many different schools of kite makers.

Kites are now made mainly in Beijing, Tianjin and Shandong in the north and Jiangsu and Zhejiang in the south.

Many of the designs and pictures of flowers, birds, insects and animals painted on the kites have symbolic meanings, such as the peony, which symbolizes riches and honour; swallow as the harbinger of spring; bat, which is a homonym of the word for "blessing"; cat and butterfly, which mean longevity. Most of the kites made in the shape of human figures are based on characters in classical Chinese novels or legends favoured by the common people, such as Monk Xuanzhuang and his three disciples: Monkey, Piggy and Sandy in the mythological novel *Journey to the West* ; the Eight Taoist Immortals who did many good things for the people; the fairy maid Magu who fermented fine wine to celebrate the birthday of Queen Mother of the West.

Kites played an important role in the progress of history. Nobody will doubt that the kite was the embryonic form of the modern spacecraft. An inscription in the Space Museum of the Smithsonian Institution in Washington D.C., USA, says that mankind's earliest flying devices were the Chinese kites and rockets.

Some Chinese historical documents have recorded the use of kites for sending man aloft and for measuring height and distance in ancient times. Kites were also used for military purposes, such as finding out how far away the enemy was and sending messages and materials.

After kites were introduced to other countries, they were put to even wider use. In 1804, an American made a kite-like flying vehicle. In 1826, a British invented a "winged vehicle" pulled by a kite. In 1874, an anonymous American crossed a 240-metre-wide canyon on a kite. In the 19th century, the French made use of a kite in a successful rescue operation at sea. All these happened before the airplane was invented.

Some Western scientists have employed kites in scientific experiments. In 1749, a Scottish man named Wilson tied thermometers on a string of six kites to measure temperature at different heights by lowering the kite slowly. The American scientist Benjamin Franklin experimented with kites in 1752 to investigate atmospheric electricity by tying a metal wire on a kite when lightning flashed and to prove that lightning in the sky and electricity generated by a generator was one and the same thing. A British meteorologist used kites to measure wind velocity in 1833 and obtained useful data. From then on, kites were used universally as tools in meteorological studies. In the early 20th century, the scientist Guglielmo Marconi used kites as antennas and successfully transmitted wireless signals across the Atlantic Ocean with Sid Jones on the other shore.

In all these scientific experiments, kites played an indispensable role. Kites will certainly continue to play a role in scientific and technological development and our daily life in the future. Kite flying is a pastime not only for the one who flies the kite, but also for those who watch it. A good kite is also a happy gift to be given to a friend or relative and to be placed at home as an ornament.

Since its invention, kite flying has gradually become a favourite pastime of the many ethnic groups in China. As folk customs and aesthetic concepts differ in different regions, the kites in different regions embody distinct features in the way they are made, shaped, decorated, painted and flown. To promote the art of kites, the kites associations in different places often conduct competitions and exchange of experience. There are now kite associations in many countries in the world. They invite one another to participate in international competitions and for exchange of experience in making kites.

The Kite Festival held in the city of Weifang in China's Shandong Province is a well-known occasion for holding competitions. It is participated by kite fans both in China and from all parts of the world. The festival has promoted the development of the art of kites both in China and other countries and fostered friendship between peoples of different countries. It has also played an important role in promoting economic growth and tourism in Weifang.

放飞
Flying a string of swallow kites.

风筝牵线建友谊　巨龙（3.5m高）风筝前面留个影
Kite-flying friends in front of the huge 3.5-metre-high head of a dragon kite.

风筝的种类

中国扎放风筝的地域很广，扎制风筝的材料和技艺有异，所以在分类上也有不同。常见的几种分类是按风筝的内容（动物、人物等）、风筝的形象（鸟、虫等）、风筝的功能（玩具、特技等）、风筝的大小（巨型、中型等）、风筝的艺术风格（传统、民间等）来划分。

现在风筝已成为一项比赛项目，为了便于比赛评比，中华全国体育运动总会曾颁布过风筝的分类、分型方法。

风筝分为八类：

一、 龙类。包括龙头、蜈蚣头等串风筝。

二、 软翅串类。就是把几只或上百只软翅风筝连接在一起。如串雁等。

三、 硬翅串类。就是把几只或上百只硬翅风筝连接在一起。如串沙燕等。

四、 板子类。凡中间和四周有竹条、骨架是平面或半立体及尾部系长穗和长绳的风筝。如八卦、人物等风筝。

五、 立体类。凡是由长、宽、厚扎成的骨架装饰而成的风筝均属此类。如宫灯、大缸等风筝。

六、 硬翅类。凡是风筝翅膀上下方均有竹条者属硬翅类。如沙燕、人物类等风筝。

七、 软翅类。凡风筝翅膀上方和中间有竹条者一般属于软翅。如鹰、蜻蜓等风筝。

八、 自由类。凡随意扎制的用新型材料或没有骨架的大小型、又不属其它类别的风筝。如用尼龙布制成的大型软体风筝等。

五型：

超大型、大型、中型、小型、微型。

北京是一座历史文化名城，放风筝有2000多年的历史了。从清末到现在北京比较知名的技艺流派有四派。其代表人物有金忠福、哈国良、马晋、孔祥泽。

金忠福的风筝造型粗犷，色彩对比鲜明。哈式风筝选材讲究，骨架坚固平整，画工精细，最为代表是"瘦沙燕"。马晋是画家，其扎制的风筝造型规整，设色雅丽，图案活泼生动，是室内很好的装饰品，其人物仙女、猴王最富特色。孔祥泽发展了曹雪芹在《南鹞北鸢考工志》收集的风筝谱，他的风筝以绘画见长。

现居住在北京的刘汉祥所扎制的风筝对传统风筝是有所发展的。刘汉祥老先生曾在中国戏曲学校、北京歌舞团任教，现任北京民间文艺家协会艺委会副主任、北京风筝协会顾问。他自幼喜欢民间艺术，精于绘画，更擅长于风筝扎制。经过四十余年的钻研，创作出北京龙、狮头蜈蚣、立体蜈蚣头等为代表的各式风筝达百余种。特别是龙头造型突破传统制法。犄角、龙须、眼眉及脑后的毛鬃均可拆装，加以设色巧妙，使其有别于其它流派龙头，这一创造受到了国内外好评。

刘先生在风筝设计上，师古而不拘古，在传统的基础上敢于创新。他先后出访过法国、日本、加拿大等国。四次赴法国表演，被授予最高荣誉奖，作品被当地博物馆收藏，并为其出版了风筝艺术专辑。其艺术成就被辑入《中国当代世界名人录》。

如今刘先生已近八十岁高龄，出于对风筝艺术的热爱，仍以精益求精的精神每日工作，不断创作出新型风筝。

Types of Kites

As kites are made and flown in vast areas and as there are differences in the materials and skills with which they are made, the way the kites are classified also differs. They are usually classified by their contents, such as animals and human figures; images, such as birds and insects; functions, such as toys and kites for special purposes; size, such as extra large and medium-sized kites; artistic style, such as traditional and folk styles.

Kite flying has also become a competitive sport. To facilitate judgement, the All-China Sports Federation has proclaimed the following way of classifying of the types and sizes of kites:

The Eight Types of Kites:

1. Dragon Kites: Strings of kites with a dragon or centipede head.

2. Soft-Wing Strings: Several or as many as 100 soft-wing kites are strung together, such as a string of swan geese.

3. Rigid-Wing Strings: Several or as many as 100 rigid-wing kites are strung together, such as a string of swallows.

4. Flat Kites: All kites with bamboo strips in the middle and on the edge, a flat surface and a long tail or line hanging from the trailing edge, such as the eight-trigrams and human figure kites.

5. Box Kites: All kites with a frame that has length, width and depth, such as kites in the shape of a palace lantern or big vat.

6. Rigid-Wing Kites: All kites with bamboo strips both above and below, such as the

swallow and human figure kites.

7. Soft-Wing Kites: All kites with bamboo strips above and in the middle, such as the eagle and dragonfly kites.

8. Free-Style Kites: Large and small kites that do not belong to the other types and made with new material or without a frame, such as the soft-bodied large kites made with nylon.

The Five Sizes of Kites:

Kites of extra large, large, medium, small and miniature sizes.

Beijing is a famous historical and cultural city with a very long kite-flying history. From the end of the Qing dynasty to the present day, there have emerged four well-known schools of kite makers, represented by Jin Zhongfu, Ha Guoliang, Ma Jin and Kong Xiangze.

Kites made by Jin Zhongfu are bold in style and painted in bright contrasty colours. The Ha-style kites are made with good materials, sturdy frames and fine decorations. His representative work is the Slim Swallow. Ma Jin was a painter. The kites made by him are regularly shaped and elegantly painted with lively designs. They are good indoor ornaments, too. The most distinguished of Ma's kites are the Fairy Maid and Monkey King. Kong Xiangze developed the styles of kites mentioned by Cao Xueqin in his *Craftsman's Manual of Southern Hawks and Northern Kites*. The kites made by Kong are noted for the pictures painted on them.

New development of the traditional kites has been made by Liu Hanxiang, who now lives in Beijing and was a teacher at the Institute of Chinese Opera and Beijing Song and Dance Ensemble. He is now vice-chairman of the Art Committee of the Beijing Association of Folk Artists and advisor to the Beijing Kite Association. Becoming interested in folk art even when he was young, he is a fine painter and skilled in making kites. After more than 40 years of study and research, he has created more than 100 different types of kites as represented by the Beijing Dragon, Dragon-Headed Centipede and Three-Dimensional Centipede Head. The Dragon Head made by him, in particular, is a breakthrough in the traditional method. The horns, whiskers, eyes, brows and bristles on the back of the head are detachable. Different from all the other styles of dragon head and cleverly painted in colour, his dragon head has been favourably received both in China and abroad.

In the design of his kites, Liu follows the traditional method but is not restricted by it. On the basis of the age-old traditions, he has made bold innovations. He has taken his kites to France, Japan, Canada and other countries, demonstrated kite-flying four times in France and awarded a prize of the highest honour. His kites have been collected and preserved in local museums. A special book about the art of his kites has been published in France. For his artistic achievements, his name has been included in the *Who's Who of the Contemporary World in China*.

Liu is nearly 80 years old, but his love for kites has not faded. He is still working every day to perfect his art and continuing to create new styles of kites.

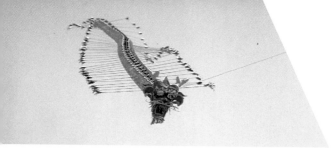

龙类
A dragon kite.

软翅串类
A string of soft-wing kites.

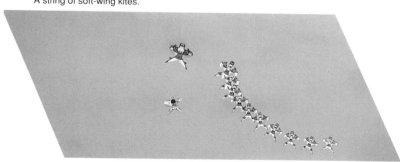

硬翅串类
A string of rigid-wing kites.

自由类

立体类
A box kite.

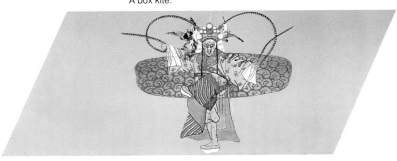

硬翅类
A rigid-wing kite.

软翅类
A soft-wing kite.

板子类
A flat kite.

龙类
Dragon Kites

制作者展示自己的作品
Kite makers display their work.

组合龙头　100cm
A composite dragon head (100 cm).

微型龙头（4cm）及串龙风筝
Miniature dragon heads (4 cm) and a dragon kite.

龙风筝
A dragon kite.

鬼脸龙头
Dragon head with an ogre face.

微型蜈蚣风筝　100cm
A miniature centipede kite (100 cm).

鬼脸蜈蚣风筝
An ogre-faced centipede kite.

放大型龙头风筝是一件很费力的事情
Flying a large dragon kite requires concerted effort.

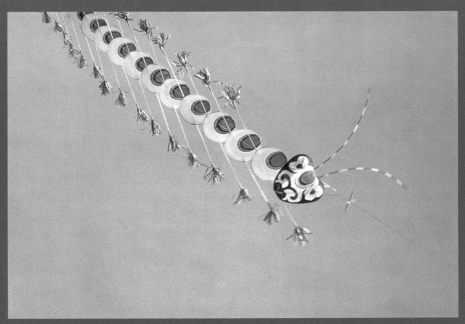

天上飞蜈蚣
A centipede in the sky.

一百余米长的龙头风筝放飞起来了
A 100-metre-long dragon kite is aloft.

软翅串类
Soft-Wing Strings of Kites

中国古典名著《西游记》中的唐僧师徒软翅串风筝
Monk Xuanzhuang and His Disciples - a string of soft-wing kites portraying characters in the classical novel *Journey to the West*.

四喜重叠
Four butterflies symbolizing "happiness."

对蝶
A pair of butterflies.

硬串类
Rigid-Wing Strings of Kites

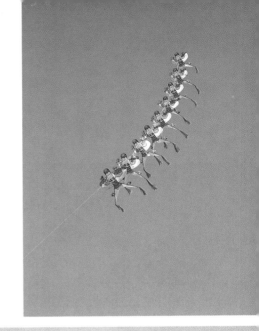

串沙燕风筝
A string of swallow kites.

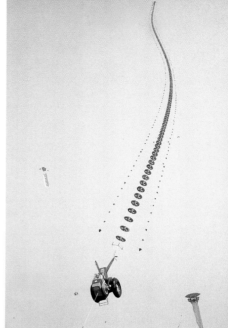

百米长的拖拉机头串风筝
A 100-metre-long string of kites
headed by a farm tractor kite.

150m 长的时装模特串风筝
A 150-metre-long string of kites of fashion models.

放串燕风筝
Flying a string of swallow kites.

立体类
Box Kites

宫灯　40 × 75cm
Palace lanterns (40 x 75 cm).

老鼠钻缸　30 × 50cm
Mouse in a Vat (30 x 50 cm).

大缸　40 × 70 cm
A big vat (40 x 70 cm).

螃蟹　90 × 50 cm
A crab kite (90 x 50 cm).

虾　60 × 40 cm
Prawn (60 x 40 cm).

自由类·特技风筝
A free-style kite made with special skill.

板子类
Flat Kites

荷瓶　65 × 85 cm
Lotus in a Vase (65 x 85 cm).

牧童　80 × 80 cm
Cowherd (80 x 80 cm).

八仙过海 60 × 75 cm
Eight Immortals Crossing the Sea (60 x 75 cm).

麒麟送子 80 × 80 cm
The Son-Delivering Unicorn (80 x 80 cm).

飞天　80 × 160 cm
Flying Celestials (80 x 160 cm).

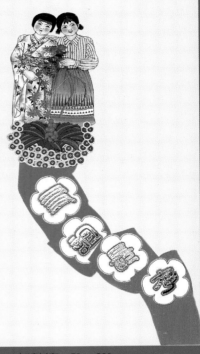

友谊长存　50 × 200 cm
Long-Lasting Friendship (50 x 200cm).

软翅类
Soft-Wing Kites

小燕　100 × 50 cm
A small swallow (100 x 50 cm).

鸽子　110 × 40 cm
Pigeon (110 x 40 cm).

黄鹂 100 × 35 cm
Oriole (100 x 35 cm).

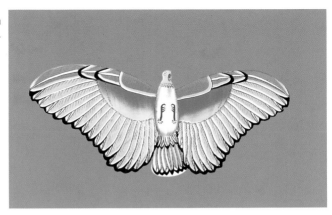

鸳鸯比翼 110 × 39 cm
A pair of mandarin ducks
(110 x 39 cm).

海鸥 100 × 40 cm
Seagull (100 x 40 cm).

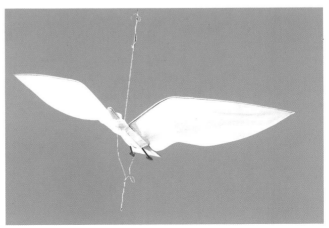

放双飞燕风筝
Flying a pair of swallow kites.

孔雀 50 × 60 cm
Peacock (50 x 60 cm).

凤凰 100 × 80 cm
Phoenix (100 x 80 cm).

寿带 250 × 200 cm
Bird of Longevity (250 x 200 cm).

鷹　350 cm
Eagle (350 cm).

鸚鵡　300 × 250 cm
Parrot (300 x 250 cm).

鶴　130 × 150 cm
Crane (130 x 150 cm).

软翅风筝中放飞鹰是比较难的，扎好的鹰风筝，拴提线是关键。
Among the soft-wing kites, the eagle is relatively more difficult to fly.
The
secret lies in correctly tying the bridle.

37

螳螂 85 × 55 cm
Mantis (85 x 55 cm).

蝉 100 × 35 cm
Cicada (100 x 35cm).

黄蜂 60 × 40 cm
Wasp (60 x 40 cm).

微型蝉 8 × 6 cm
A miniature cicada (8 x 6 cm).

放飞黄蜂翅翼发出嗡嗡响声
The wasp buzzes in the air.

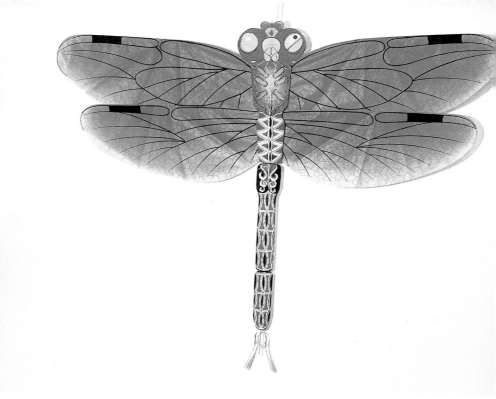

绿蜻蜓　120 × 95 cm　Green dragonfly (120 x 95 cm).

白蜻蜓　100 × 70 cm
White dragonfly (100 x 70 cm).

微型蜻蜓　8 × 6 cm
A miniature dragonfly (8 x 6 cm).

蜻蜓式风筝放远而放不高
Dragonfly kites can fly far but not high.

紫蝴蝶　80 × 26 cm
Purple butterfly (80 x 26 cm).

小蝴蝶　60 × 35 cm
Small butterfly (60 x 35 cm).

翠蝴蝶
Green butterfly.

五虾图 90 × 65 cm Five Prawns (90 x 65 cm).

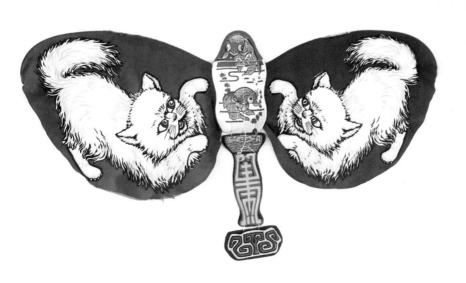

双猫戏鱼 90 × 60 cm Two Cats Toying with a Fish (90 x 60 cm).

风筝也是儿童很喜欢的玩具
Kites are children's favourite toys.

京剧脸谱
Painted face -- a character in a Peking opera.

玉皇大帝　95 × 55 cm
The Great Jade Emperor (85 x 55 cm).

刘海戏蟾　80 × 150 cm
Liu Hai Playing with a Toad (80 x 150 cm).

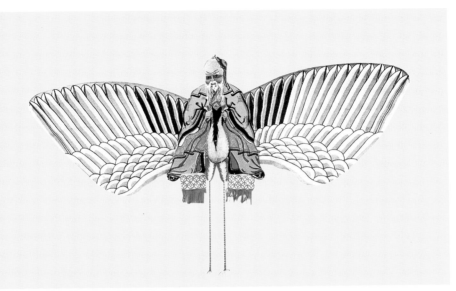

老寿星　90 × 70 cm
God of Longevity (90 x 70 cm).

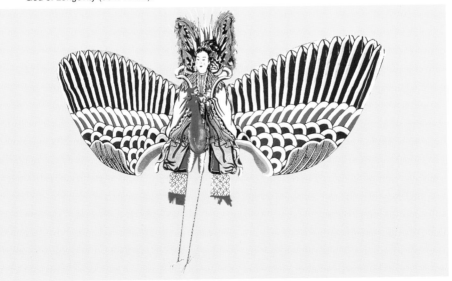

麻姑骑凤，中国传说中的仙女，以灵芝酿酒，每年农历三月三，为王母祝寿。90 × 40 cm
Ma Gu Riding on a Phoenix (90 x 40 cm). Ma Gu is an immortal in a Chinese fairy tale who ferments ganoderma wine and offers it to Queen Mother Wang on the latter's birthday on the third day of the third lunar month every year.

中国古典名著《封神演义》人物——雷震子　100 × 45 cm
Lei Zhen Zi (100 x 45 cm), a character in the famous classical novel *Canonization of Gods*

仙鹤童子　50 × 30 cm
Boy and Crane (50 x 30 cm).

梁祝 98 × 49 cm
Liang Shanbo and Zhu Yingtai, two lovers in a Shaoxing opera (98 x 49 cm).

组合风筝孔雀开屏　350 × 300 cm
Peacocks Displaying Feathers, a composite kite (350 × 300 cm).

葫芦万代　200 × 150 cm
Calabash of Longevity (200 x 150 cm)

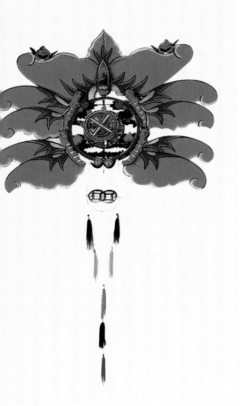

五蝠捧寿　100 × 150 cm
Longevity and Five Bats (100 x 150 cm)

群鸟祝贺 300 × 250 cm
Birds Offering Congratulations (300 x 250 cm)

八仙庆寿　150 × 160 cm
Eight Immortals Celebrating a Birthday (150 x 160 cm).

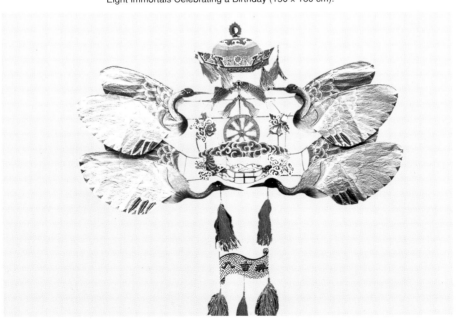

八吉祥　120 × 120 cm
Eight Signs of Good Luck (120 x 120 cm).

"百花齐放" 单飞
"A Hundred Flowers Blossom."

硬翅类
Rigid-Wing Kites

中国民间传说中驱妖逐邪之神——钟馗。 100 × 85 cm
Zhong Kui (100 x 85 cm). a god for expelling evil spirits in folk
legend.

猴王，中国古典名著《西游记》中的神猴　120 × 160 cm
Monkey (120 x 160 cm), a character in the mythological novel *Journey to the West*.

时迁偷鸡，中国古典名著《水浒》中的神偷手　80 × 60 cm
Shi Qian Stealing a Chicken (80 x 60 cm). Shi Qian is a smart burglar in the classical novel *Outlaws of the Marsh*.

仙女采药　160 × 150 cm
A Fairy Maiden Gathering Medicinal Herbs (160 x 150 cm).

观音送子　125 × 120 cm
Guanyin Delivering a Son (125
x 120 cm).

哪吒闹海，传说中的神仙，为报打不
平，抽了龙子的筋。120 × 80 cm
Ne Zha Causes Havoc in the Sea (120 x
80 cm). Ne Zha is a god in folk legend
who removes the tendons of the Dragon
King's son in defence of justice.

水漫金山。神话故事中白蛇精为救被法海和尚关在金山寺的丈夫，用河水及虾兵虾将在金山战斗。140 × 110 cm
Flooding the Golden Hill (140 x 110 cm). To rescue her husband who was imprisoned by Monk Fa Hai in the Temple of Golden Hill, the White Snake Spirit in a fairy tale mobilized shrimp soldiers and crab generals to flood the temple with river waters.

龙寿燕　300 × 250 cm
A swallow kite decorated with dragons for longevity (300 x 250 cm).

青蛙燕　70 × 65 cm
A swallow kite with a frog decoration (70 x 65 cm).

百蝠骈臻　70 × 65 cm
A swallow kite decorated with bats (70 x 65 cm).

五蝠瘦燕　75 × 90 cm
A slim swallow decorated with five bats (75 x 90 cm).

聚蝼蝈 70 × 80 cm
Mole Cricket and Snails (70 x 80 cm).

子鱼卧年 30 × 45 cm
Baby and Fish for a Year of Abundance. (35 x 45 cm).

花王　150 × 150 cm
Peony, the King of Flowers (150 x 150 cm).

福寿双全　150 × 230 cm
Happiness and Longevity (150 x 230 cm).

八仙庆寿　150 × 80 cm
Eight Immortals Celebrating
a Birthday (150 x 80 cm).

放飞燕风筝
Flying swallow kites.

北京刘汉祥先生经四十余年钻研创作出龙、狮头蜈蚣、立体蜈蚣头等为代表的风筝百余种。
特别是龙头造型突破传统制法，犄角、龙须、眼眉及脑后毛鬃均可拆装。这里向读者展示
其制作的几款风筝。

Liu Hanxiang has been making kites for over 40 years. Among the more than 100 types of his works
are centipedes with a dragon or lion head and box kites with a centipede head. The dragon heads
made by him have detachable horns, whiskers, eyes, brows and bristles, which is a breakthrough in
the traditional design. He is here displaying one of his kites.

刘先生制作的组合龙头，大龙头 1m，小龙头 4 cm。
A large composite dragon head (1 metre) and a small composite
dragon head (4 cm) made by Liu Hanxiang.

刘先生制作的组合五龙燕 250 × 120 cm
A swallow kite with five dragons on it (250 x 120 cm) made by Liu.

刘先生制作的鹰风筝
局部　鹰为 350. cm
Detail of an eagle kite
made by Liu (350 cm).

刘先生制作的虎年喜鹊报春　130 × 200 cm
Magpies Heralding Spring, a kite made by Liu for the year of the Tiger (130 x 200 cm).

刘先生制作的组合美国公牛队风筝　180 × 250 cm
A composite kite of the American Bull basketball team made by Liu (180 x 250 cm).

刘先生制作的组合福寿风筝　150 × 250 cm
Happiness and Longevity, a composite kite made by Liu (150 x 250 cm).

刘先生制作的降龙伏虎风筝　160 × 120 cm
Subduing a Dragon and Defeating a Tiger, a kite made by Liu (160 x 120 cm).

风筝的放飞

　　放风筝首先要准备好线。线是根据风筝的大小来确定其粗细和长短。大风中放巨型风筝，要用直径3-5厘米粗的缆绳，而放微型风筝，线可细如发丝。线的长度，短则几米，长则上千米。线的质地可以是麻线、棉线、丝线、尼龙线。最好的是丝线，但其价较贵。

　　放风筝的线准备好后，要用一个器具把它绕起来。这个器具叫"桄子"。桄子的大小由线的粗细长短来确定。桄子种类有拐子形的，手摇园盘形的，有由中间有六条细棍和两边各有一个舵轮及中间有一轴棍组成的等等。当然放不太大的风筝，也可把线绕到一根小圆棍上，但放飞时，收放线不方便。

　　把线拴在风筝的提线（顶线）上，只要有风，风筝就可放飞起来。因为风筝只有在空气中运行，产生的升力大于自然的重力后，它才能飞上天。所以一年四季，只要有风，就能放风筝。风力的大小与风筝关系很大。一般来说。当风力在2－6级时，匀可以放风筝。2－3级风适合放面积在0.1－0.5平方米的风筝，如放飞软翅的鸟、虫风筝。当风力为3－4级，可以放飞面积为1平方米左右的各种风筝。风力达到5－6级时，可以放面积达2平方米以上的各种大型风筝。

　　一只合格的风筝，放飞起来并不难。只要风力合适，随手撒出风筝，牵放引线，风筝就会慢慢升高。开始时会有稍微的摇摆，随不断地收线、放线，风筝逐渐升起来，并平衡地飘在高空。若风筝在空中左右打晃或打转，首先要检查风筝左右两翼骨架是否对称。若两翼没问题，就是提线（顶线）拴得不好。风筝往前俯冲可把提线上调；风筝左倾可把提线右调，这样就可把风筝放起。初放风筝最好两人，一人拿着桄子放线，一人拿着风筝跑出十几米外，迎风高举风筝放手，拿桄子的人即时拉动引线风筝就起来了。放稍大些的风筝最好戴上手套。因为有时风力较大时，风筝会急速上升，线放得快，就会把手拉破。

　　有些人放风筝时带个"送饭"。"送饭"是一种特制的风筝。它设置一装有机关的小盒，盒内放些花瓣或彩色纸屑。把"送饭"挂在风筝的牵引线上，"送饭"就立刻沿引线飞上去，碰到风筝后，"送饭"的机关就打开，装在盒内的花瓣或彩色纸屑就撒落天空，像天女散花，很好看。也有的挂串小灯，从盒内放出，挂在夜空，像闪烁的星星。这些都增加了放风筝的情趣。

扎放风筝，所以被人们喜好，是因为扎放风筝可以陶冶人们的情操。好的风筝，形象优美，绘画精制，色彩艳丽，不但飞到天上好看悦目，挂在家中也是一种很别致的装饰品。自己亲手扎制的风筝，也是馈赠亲朋好友的珍贵礼品。

放风筝的人们，沐浴着阳光，在野外呼吸着新鲜空气，吐故纳新，舒展四肢筋骨，促进血液循环，有助于促进新陈代谢，增强身体健康。

放风筝时，手臂要动，腿脚要奔跑移动，眼睛要仰望远视，享受着运动的乐趣。放风筝还有利于驱除疲劳、健脑益智，对治疗神经抑郁症、视力减退，尤其是对长年从事脑力劳动，伏案工作的人们有利，不但提高了人们的抗病能力，而且对颈椎及腰病的治疗，都是极其有利的。多晒太阳可以促进身体对钙的吸收，总比吃补钙药划算。

在国外也是越来越多的人们利用放风筝来锻炼身体。放风筝的医疗作用，越来越被人们所重视。国外很多国家成立了风筝医院和疗养院，应用"风筝疗法"对一些病症已取得了明显的治疗效果。

随着人们生活水平的提高和休闲日的增加，为丰富多彩的精神生活，风筝将会发挥更大的作用。

提醒大家注意的是：城市内放风筝时，一定要远离高压线和机场，在立交桥上放飞，也要注意安全。

Kite Flying

A string, or line, has to be properly attached to a kite before flying it. The length and thickness of the string are determined by the size of the kite. To fly an extra large kite in a strong wind requires a string of 3-5 millimeters in thickness. The string for flying a miniature kite is as thin as hair. The length of the string can be a few metres or as long as 1,000 metres. The string can be one of hemp, cotton, silk or nylon. A silk string is the best, though it is more expensive.

The string is wound around a winder, the size of which is determined by the length and thickness of the string. The winder usually consists of a roller that turns on an axis with a handle. To fly a small kite, the string can be wound on a small stick, which, however, is not as convenient as a winder for paying out the string.

The string is attached to the kite by the bridle, which is usually composed of three cords forming an inverted triangle. The kite will fly only when the lift force of the wind is greater than the natural force of gravity. Kites can fly in all the four seasons of the year as long as there is wind of force 2-6 on the Beaufort scale. A force 2-3 wind is good for flying a kite of 0.1-0.5 square metre, such as the soft-wing bird and insect kites; a force 3-4 wind, for a kite of about 1 square metre; a force 5-6 wind, for a large kite of more than 2 square metres.

A properly made kite is not difficult to fly. In a suitable wind, it will rise to the sky when the flier pays out the line. The kite may swing slightly at first, which can be adjusted by paying out or drawing in the string. If the kite tumbles the left or right or rotates in the air, it is necessary to check the wing frames of the kite. If the wings are symmetrical and properly balanced, the trouble is caused by the bridle. If the kite dives forward, shorten the two higher cords of the bridle. If the kite swings to the left or right, adjust the bridle to the opposite direction. For a beginner, the best way to fly a kite is by a team of two persons, with one holding the kite against the wind and high above his head and the other holding the string winder and standing at least 10 metres away from the kite. When the holder lets go the kite, the other should pull in the string. The kite will be sent aloft. When the wind is strong, it is advisable to wear a pair of gloves to prevent the string from cutting the hand when the flier paying out the string at a higher speed. Some kite fliers attach a small gadget known as Songfan (food deliverer) to the kite. This Songfan is a specially made kite in the shape of a box with a catch on it and with colourful fragments of paper inside the box. When the Songfan climbs up the string to the kite, the box will open and scatter the fragments of paper in the sky like the mythical Heavenly Maid Scattering Flowers. There can also be a string of lights in the Songfan, which will hang down from the kite like stars in the sky and add interest to kite flying.

Making and flying kites is favoured by people because it exerts a favourable influence on a person's character. A beautifully shaped kite painted with pictures in bright colour is not only a pleasant object to look at as it rises into the sky, but also an unusual ornament on the wall at home. A kite made by oneself is a precious gift to be given to a friend or relative.

Kite flying is a good exercise. Bathing in sunlight and breathing the fresh air of an open field, a kite flyer will find that flying a kite is a good opportunity to exercise the limbs, promote blood circulation and metabolism and improve one's health as a whole.

As one has to move the arms and legs constantly and to keep one's eyes at the kite in the air in order to enjoy the fan of the pastime, flying a kite is a good way to drive away fatigue and invigorate the brain and a good cure for those suffering from nervous depression and weakened eyesight. It is a good exercise particularly for those engaged in mental work over long periods at the desk because kite flying can improve one's resistance to disease in general and cure ailments of the vertebrae cervicales and the back in particular. Exposure to the sun will improve absorption of calcium, which is better than taking calcium tablets.

More and more people in other countries are engaged in kite flying as a physical exercise. The curative effect of kite flying has also attracted people's attention. There are now kite-flying hospitals and sanitoria in some countries, where the "kite-flying therapy" has achieved successful curative effects.

As people's living standards improve and as there is now more time for leisure, kites will play a more interesting role in enriching people's life.

However, kite fliers are to be warned that when flying a kite in the city, it important to keep away from high-tension transmission lines and an airfield. It is also necessary to pay attention to safety when flying a kite on a overpass.

放风筝首先要准备好桄子和线，桄子的种类很多，风筝商店均有出售，但有些桄子价格较高，不妨自己动手制作。放风筝的大小种类不同，因用的线（绳）粗细不同，收线（绳）的方法就不同，所以桄子就有差别。不管用什么桄子，把风筝能顺利放出和收回，线（绳）又不乱成一团，用什么桄子都可以。放风筝的线（绳），可用丝线、棉线、麻线、尼龙线。丝线（绳）最好，但价高。

A long string and a string winder are necessary for flying a kite. There are many types of winders for different types of kites and different lines (strings). The purpose of using a winder is to prevent the line from getting entangled. The flyer's line can be silk, cotton, hemp or nylon. The silk line is the best though it is more expensive.

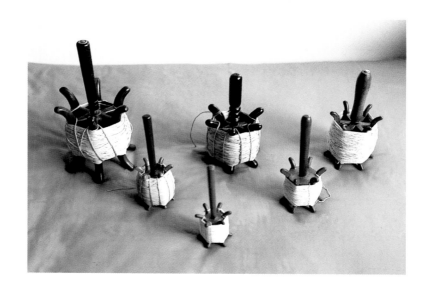

放小型风筝用的桄子
Winder for flying a small kite.

放中型风筝用的桄子
Winder for flying a medium-
sized kite.

放大型风筝用的桄子
Winder for flying a large kite.

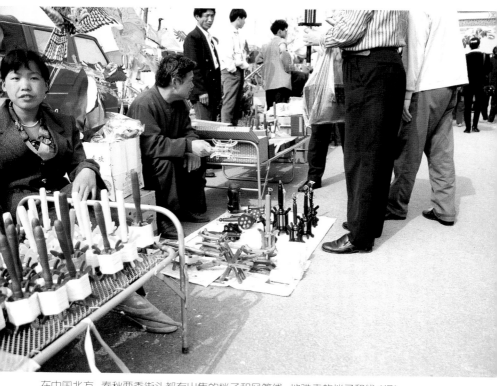

在中国北方，春秋两季街头都有出售的桄子和风筝线。地难卖的桄子和线（绳）价钱便宜，但质量差些，用于放中小型风筝还是可以的。

Winders and strings for flying kites are sold by vendors on the street in the northern part of China in spring and autumn. They are inexpensive and good enough for flying small and medium-sized kites.

很多工艺商店都有销售放飞风筝的用品，质量也好。
Good-quality kite flying gear is available in many arts and crafts shops.

要放风筝，首先把风筝带到放飞点，风筝准备好后，就要拴牵引线（绳）。线一定要拴好，拴线（绳）的原则是一要牢固，二要好解开。
Before flying a kite, the flier's line is to be tied to the bridle. The flier's line should be tied firmly and can be untied easily.

拴牵引线（绳）前首先要检查一下原先拴的提（顶）线是否牢固和合适，
然后再拴牵引线（绳）。

Before tying the flier's line, it is necessary to see if the bridle is properly adjusted.

提线符合放飞标准就要拴好牵引线，牵引线一定要拴牢固，防止风筝在
放飞中脱线而飞，造成遗憾。

It is important to tie the flier's line firmly to the bridle to prevent the kite from
breaking away.

牵引线（绳）拴牢固后，检查拴的是否对称合适，有偏差就要调整，否则上天后就会左右摇摆，飞不上天。

After tying the flier's line to the bridle, check if the bridle is properly adjusted. Otherwise, the kite will swing to the left or right and cannot go up.

拴引线（绳）不但要拴的牢，还要好解开，不然收风筝时，牵引线解不开会损坏提线，造成麻烦。没有桄子，绕成线团的牵引线，一定要注意防止缠成乱麻。

The flier's line is to be tied to the bridle in a knot that can be easily untied. Otherwise, the bridle may be damaged when untying the flier's line. When flying a kite without a winder, it is important to prevent the string from getting tangled.

放飞前的一切工作准备好后，就可放飞，当然首先要有风。一个人放飞风筝，首先要使风筝迎风而起，然后慢慢放线，有时也需收线。放线、收线快慢要根据风的大小而定。风筝在迎风中虽然会左右摇摆，但它会慢慢升高。

There must be wind for flying a kite. The flier is to run with the kite against the wind to send the kite aloft while paying out the line slowly. Pulling in or paying out the line is decided by the force of the wind. The kite may swing to the left or right, but it will gradually ascend to the sky.

风筝飞上天，眼望天空，根据风力大小和风向不同，要不断的调整牵引线。
The flier is to keep his eyes on the kite and adjust the line according to the force and direction of the wind.

一个人最容易放的风筝是蝶类软翅风筝。
Soft-wing kites like the butterfly kites are the easiest to fly by a single person.

两个人放风筝就要比一个人放飞容易多了。
It is much easier to fly a kite by a team of two persons.

两人放风筝，一人迎风高举风筝与拿牵引线者相距5米外，听到"放"立刻撒手。
When flying a kite by two persons, one of them is to hold the kite high against the wind. When the other holding the winder and standing five metres away, says, "Let go," he is to let go the kite immediately.

拿桄子的人，发出"放"后，看见拿风筝者撒手，就立刻拉线，风筝就会升起来，或是牵引者迎风慢跑，不断收放线，风筝就会越飞越高。
The holder of the winder is then to pull in the line immediately. He can also run against the wind with the kite behind him until the kite begins to fly.

放风筝因收线不当、也就是收线过快或是没有用桄子、把收回的线搞乱成一团、再把牵引线解开是比较麻烦的。

When drawing in the line, do it slowly and use a winder. It is important to prevent the line from getting tangled.

放飞龙或串一类的风筝，首先要把风筝的串翅平摆在地面，使其各翅互不缠绕，当风力适合时才能放飞。

When flying a dragon or other strings of kites, the many body kites should be laid neatly on the ground to see that they are not tangled.

放飞龙或串一类风筝，摆平后要检查牵引线(绳)是否拴牢，因串风筝上天后兜风力是很大的，当风力合适时把串风筝抬起，有一人指挥准备放飞。

It is important to tie the flier's line firmly to the bridle of a string of kites because a string of kites has a very strong pulling force. It takes several persons to fly a string of kites with one person taking overall command.

放飞龙串风筝在统一指挥下，把抬起的风筝先放尾部使其迎风而起，要拽好龙头，当其身全部腾空后，就要根据风力决定放线(绳)的速度和长度。

Under unified command, the person holding the tail of a string of kites is to let go the tail first and then followed by the others. When the whole string is in the air, the flier is to draw in or let out the line according to the force of the wind.

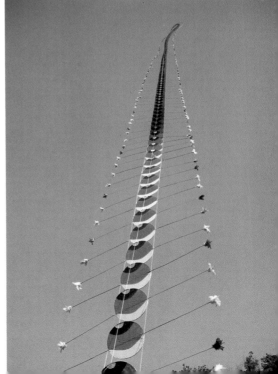

龙串风筝飞上天空，可一人或几人用手拉线（绳）操纵，也可拴在一木桩上或其它重物上，风筝在天空飘荡。

When a dragon kite is in the sky, the line can be manipulated by one or several persons. It can also be tied to a pole or a heavy object to let the kite float in the air by itself.

风筝在天上，你可坐在小橙上，可根据风的情况，随时对风筝进行调整，几个人一起聊聊风筝的趣事，真是惬意。

When the kite is in the sky, the flier can take easy and sit on a stool to adjust the line and chat with other fliers. Kite flying will then be a really pleasurable pastime.

放稍大一些的风筝，飞上天后，就得几个人拽着，根据风向要不断的调整自己的站位，这样才能保证风筝平稳飞在天空。

When a larger kite rises into the sky, the line has to be steadied by several persons to keep the kite in balance.

放对蝶也要几个人才行，不然风筝提线绞在一起就麻烦了。
It takes several persons to fly a pair of butterflies to prevent their bridles from becoming entangled.

风筝的大小无从统计，图中群众围的这一巨龙风筝头 3.5 米多高，身长 555 米，它一字摆开，尾部在山坡上，放飞时用步话机指挥。

There is no record of the largest size of kites. The head of the dragon kite in this picture is 3.5 metres high and its body, 555 metres long. While the head lies on level ground, its body extends to the top of a slope. It requires walkie-talkies to direct the take-off of the kite.

巨龙飞筝起飞，需要6级以上的风力才行，风力小风筝很难飞起来。
An extra large cannot fly unless there is a force 6 wind.

起飞的巨龙风筝牵引绳直径为4cm粗的尼龙绳，它拴在汽车绞盘上，为了加重汽车的重量，车上站满了人。
The flier's line of the extra large kite is a 4 cm-thick nylon rope. It is wound on the winch of a motor vehicle with many people standing on it the increase its weight.

放风筝是一项很好的体育运动，所以能吸引人。
Kite flying is a good sport participated by many people.

春天天气不冷不热，又多偏东风和南风，气流稳定上升，水平方向的风力又不
很大，风筝很容易上升，所以是放风筝的好时机。

Spring is an ideal season for flying kites because the weather is neither too cold nor too
hot and there is often wind from the east or south with steady rising currents. Since the
wind moving parallel to the ground is not strong, it is very easy for the kite to rise.

春天放风筝，对人体健康是很有益处，沐浴阳光春风，有"疏泄内热、增强体质之益"。
Flying a kite in spring is believed to be good for "relieving the internal body heat and building up health."

放风筝的地方也是展示和出售自制风筝的好地方。
A kite-flying place is a good spot for displaying and selling home-made kites.

放风筝使人情绪开朗，心境愉快，是消疲劳的最好运动。
Kite flying is one of the best sports for cheering up oneself and relieving fatigue.

看别人放飞在天上的风筝，也是一种艺术享受。
Kite-watching is also a good diversion.

放风筝是一个十分大众化的体育运动，它投资少，又吸引人。放风筝处，观看者的兴趣不比放风筝者差。看别人放风筝一样可以活动颈椎，改善视力，消除眼睛疲惫。

Kite flying is a popular mass sport which requires only a small investment and is attractive to people of all ages. Even kite watching is a good diversion for exercising the cervical vertebra, improving eyesight and relieving eye strain.

风筝飞上天，天、地、人融为一体，触目皆景，美不胜收。

With kites in the sky and people on the ground, heaven, earth and people present a beautiful picture everywhere.

儿童喜欢花花绿绿的风筝，皆因儿童好动、看着大人放的风筝上天，他们也想一展身手，跑跑跳跳的拉着风筝飞起来，他们多么高兴。吐故纳新，吸着新鲜空气，促进了血流循环，这对儿童是多么好的运动。

Kites are favourite toys for children, too. They often come with the grown-up to fly kites. It is a good exercise for them to breathe in plenty of fresh air.

每个家庭不管人口多少，除了放风筝这一运动能统一行动外，任何体育运动在一个家
庭要统一行动，恐怕有点难。节假日全家上公园散心，放一放风筝是一件很开心的事。
Families often come out together to fly kites. Kite flying is easier than any other undertakings for
a family to take united action. Flying a kite in a park on a holiday is certainly a happy occasion for
the whole family.

春季家庭成员，约上亲朋好友一起到郊外放风筝，既锻炼了身体，又增加友谊，尤其对老年人来说是一件大好事。

Going to the countryside to fly a kite together with family members, friends and relatives is not only a good exercise, but also an occasion for improving understanding. It is particularly good for older people.

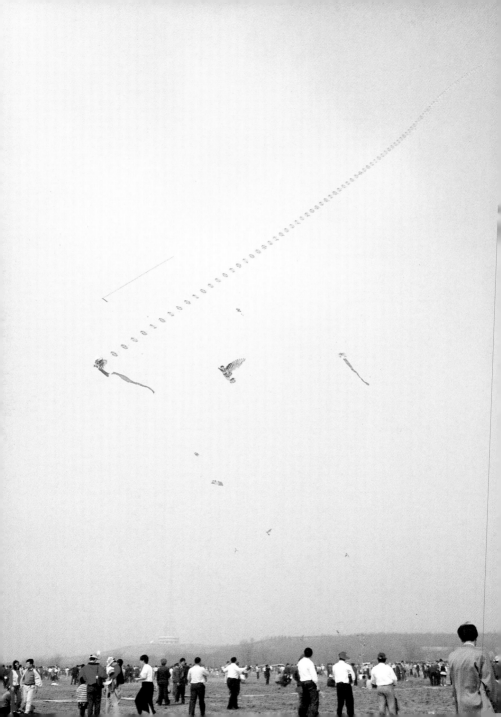

放风筝最好在野外和农村，障碍少，电线少，而且空气也好，空间大，奔跑移动方便。在城市空间小，放风筝障碍多，当然也有放风筝的地方，如高楼之间、立交桥和边缘地区。市区最好的放飞区是公园或广场。北京天安门广场就是放风筝的好地方。

The best place for flying a kite is the countryside or an open field where there are few obstacles or electric wires and plenty of space to run around. In the cities, people can only fly kites between tall buildings, at a pass-over, in a park or square. Tian An Men Square in Beijing is a good place for flying kites.

有些人放风筝时带个"送饭"，它实际上是一种特制的小型风筝。"送饭"大部分造型为蝴蝶，也叫"碰蝶"。"送饭"设有一机关装置的小盒，内装花瓣或彩色纸屑，把"送饭"挂在风筝牵引线上，风就把它送上天，它和风筝一碰，小盒就打开，花瓣或彩色纸屑就撒落天空，像天女散花十分好看，也有放出一小串小灯，傍晚时在天上像闪烁的星星，这些都是增加放风筝的情趣。

Kite fliers sometimes send a Songfan up to the sky along the kite string. A Songfan is a specially made small kite attached to the flier's line by hooks. As it is often made in the shape of a butterfly, it is also called "knocking butterfly." There is a catch in the small box on the Songfan. When the Songfan goes up and hits the kite, the box will open and scatter flower petals or colourful fragments of paper like the Heavenly Maiden Scattering Flowers. A Songfan can also carry a string of small lights, which will twinkle like stars in the sky and add interest to kite flying.

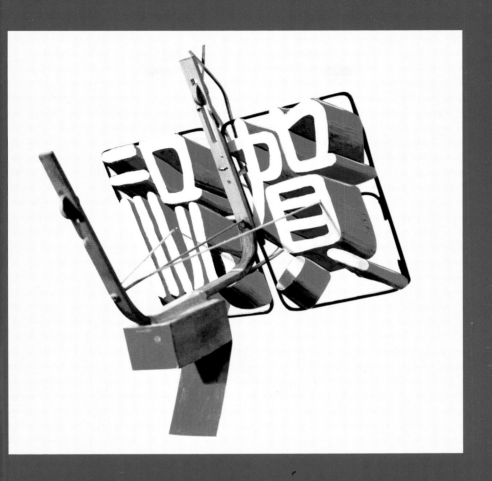

放风筝不仅可以自娱、娱人，制作精良、绘画独特的好风筝，还是馈赠亲朋好友的珍贵礼品，也可陈列于宾馆饭店和家中供欣赏和装饰环境。

A finely made kite is a good gift for a friend or relative. It can also be hung in a hotel, restaurant or home as an ornament.

自从风筝产生后，经过长时期的流传、风筝在扎制造型、装饰、绘画及放飞技巧上都形成了各自的特色，为了宏扬发展风筝艺术，中国各地的风筝协会经常举行风筝比赛。现在世界上很多国家也有风筝协会，为了更大的交流，各国互相邀请国外的风筝爱好者参加风筝比赛，以促进世界风筝的更大发展。

After long years of continuous improvement, kite makers have developed their own styles and features in making, decorating, painting the kites and the skills of flying them. To promote the art of kite making, kite associations in the various places in China often sponsor kite competitions. For exchanging experience and promoting further development, kite associations in many countries often invite kite lovers from different parts of the world to take part in competitions.

中国天津魏元泰先生选送风筝参加 1915 年巴拿马赛会，并获金质奖章。
Kites made by Wei Yuantai in Tianjin won a gold medal at the Panama Exposition in1915.

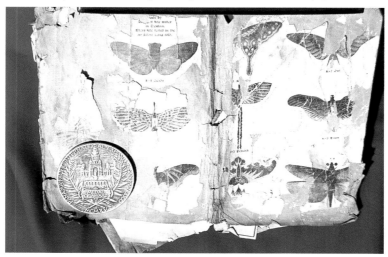

中国山东省潍坊风筝节在国内外是一项比较有影响的风筝比赛。每年四月中旬，潍坊都举办国际风筝比赛。各类放飞的风筝都进行评比。风筝节不但邀请国内扎制风筝名家参加，而且邀请国际风筝爱好者参加。

The Kite Festival held in Weifang, Shandong Province, in mid-April every year and participated by kite makers and kite fans from all parts of the world is an important kite event both in China and the world.

这是被邀请参加潍坊风筝节比赛的国外代表队，他们不但带来了制作风筝和放飞技巧，而且带来了各国的友谊。

Teams from other countries have brought to Weifang not only their kites and kite-flying skills, but also friendship.

年龄并不是放风筝的障碍。
Age makes no difference in flying a kite.

白天未尽趣，晚上接着放。
Kites continue to fly at night.

边放边交流，技艺更高一筹。
Exchanging experience and skills.

一根银线牵友谊，互相交流，语言障碍并不重要了。
Difference in language is unimportant for making friends and exchanging experience.

有困难找民警，这位女士可找对了，要民警帮助解放放飞中遇到的麻烦。
A policeman comes to the help of a lady whose kite has got into trouble.

参观中国风筝
Viewing Chinese kites.

留个纪念
Taking a photograph
as a memento.

138

银线牵友谊，友谊代代传
Long-lasting friendship.

潍坊销售风筝的商店、地滩随处可见
There are many shops selling kites in Weifang.

买个中国风筝带回去
Buy a kite and take it home.

风筝的制作

一、制作风筝首先要准备好所需工具：钢锯、木锉、电工刀、劈刀、平刃刀、斜刃刀、尖嘴钳、钻、酒精灯或腊烛、麻线或棉线、浆糊或胶水、剪子、锤子、熨斗、焊枪、焊锡、焊油、针、尺子、铅笔、圆规等。

二、准备材料。扎风筝的骨架用料主要是竹子，也可用机制木条、塑料和金属骨架。根据需要可分别准备些拉力强的薄纸、塑料薄膜、绢、真丝绸和尼龙绸。还要备些薄铜片、剪开的易拉罐皮及不同型号的铅丝。

三、扎制风筝，首先要有风筝的设计图，要准确的画好风筝骨架和画样图。最好放成和所制风筝大小一样的图纸（巨型、大型风筝图应按比例缩小，这样制作时比划着图纸下料扎制，作出的风筝准确无误，便于一次成功。

四、制作风筝骨架。扎风筝骨架竹子最好（这里只介绍扎制竹子骨架），它轻、强度和韧性匀好，易烤弯曲。按设计图所需尺寸取料，尽量取两竹节之间的竹子，因竹节不宜烤弯曲，若取材长，不好去掉竹节时，竹节要锉平，烤弯时要分外谨慎。选竹时应选老竹和干竹。青竹、湿竹放置一年以后才能使用。朽竹根本不能用。

A、选好竹子后，把截好的竹子锉平，用刀劈成风筝骨架所需竹的宽度，再用刀削成所要求的厚度，然后用刀刮平。

B、烤弯。在设计的风筝中，会有很多的圆弧和圆圈，这就需要在高温灯上将竹子烤弯。首先用双手拿着竹条的两端，在酒精灯或腊烛上方烤。烤时应注意竹皮的方向。一般烤时皮朝上，这样弹性强，也有按设计要求烤时皮朝下。弯烤时，不要急，注意竹子烤得油脂溢出，也叫"出汗"，这时立即弯出所需要的弧度来。若不等烤出油是弯不过来的，强行弯就会断裂，即使弯过来，冷却后也会弹回去。而且注意不能烤得过火，过火就会糊、焦、干，是很易断裂的。

C、把烤好的竹子用平刃刀在竹子截面的对等处，一劈两半，成为对称的两条骨架材料。在劈竹料进刀时，进刀的速度一定要慢，不要一刀劈到底，不然就会使竹条裂缝向一边偏斜，使两半不对称，或是其中一条断裂。在进刀慢的基础上，还要随时调整刀刃的方向。刀刃一般调向竹面厚的竹条，再慢慢向下进刀。

D、进行扎制。为了使结合的两部分完全吻合，将劈开的两根竹条并排对准，用斜刀削出一斜度，把其中一根竹条翻过，即可用线绑扎。绑扎时，线一定要排列整齐，而且要绑紧。一些部分也可以用铜片或铝片焊成大小一样的金属套筒，把两条竹条连接起来。组合风筝多采用此法。

五、绘画。给风筝绘画着色，这是制作好风筝必不可少的。扎制的风筝不同，绘画也不一样。作者可根据不同形式的风筝，创造出多种不同色彩的风筝。彩绘风筝，根据风筝的不同，而采取的形式也有所不同。有的是把绘画好的图纸裱糊到扎好的骨架上，就是先绘后糊；也有的是糊好风筝后，在风筝上绘画，这是先糊后绘；也有的是在糊好的风筝部分地方绘画，一部分是绘好后，再糊上去。山东潍坊过去有把木板年画糊上去，色泽艳丽，十分悦目。

六、熨平。把糊风筝的裱料，按需要裁好，有的需要绘画的着好色，用熨斗把所有的用料每件都要熨平整，便于裱糊。熨时温度不能太高。

七、糊。在扎好在骨架上涂上胶或浆糊，把熨平的纸（绢等）料，绷紧糊上。也有的把纸、绢等裱料喷潮，这样糊到骨架上，晾干后会绷得很紧。要特别注意，糊时两膀兜要深浅一致，松紧要适中。

八、组装。把全部制好的风筝配件组合在一起，拴好提线（顶线），风筝就算扎制好了。拴提线是十分重要的，它关系到风筝是否能很好地飞上天。风筝不同，所以风筝的提线多少，也是有差别的。

拴一根提线，要注意上、下、左、右的移动调整，使风筝平衡。一根提线是比较难拴。如鹰就是一根提线。

二根提线拴法是上、下移动，调整上下提线的长度，达到风筝的平衡。如软翅风筝中的蜻蜓、蝶类等。

三根提线拴法是两根提线的发展，它可以控制风筝纵向、横向的平稳。这是风筝提线最常见的一种拴法。三根提线一般作对称状，上二下一，上线左右相等，下线比上线略长，使提线的中心高于风筝重心 1－2 厘米。风筝向一方侧，可调反向提线。三根提线风筝，如沙燕。

拴四根以上或多达百根以上提线的风筝，一般都是大型和巨型风筝、硬拍子和立体风筝。这类风筝骨架多，面积大，在大风中放飞，所以提线要使其各部受力均匀，每根提线要松紧一致，总的角度要适合。俗话说"提线拴得好，风筝飞得高。"

九、试飞。扎好的风筝，拴好提线，在室外要进行试飞。在放飞中调整不适合的地方，使风筝能平稳飞上天。然后把试飞好的风筝收入盒内或陈列在室内。再次在外放飞时，拴好牵引线就可放飞，免得到时放飞不起来。

十、收藏。试飞调整好的风筝一定要收藏好。装饰性较强的风筝，可以挂于室内墙壁上，这是一种很好的装饰品。也可把较大的风筝挂于通风处，防止发霉、虫蛀及压坏。把小一些的风筝装入箱内和纸盒内，并放入防潮剂和防蛀剂。只要珍惜收藏，风筝是可以保存很久的。

Making Kites

1. Tools required: Hacksaw, saw, wood file, electrician's knife, hatchet, straight-edged knife, diagonal-edged knife, round-nose pliers, drill, alcohol burner or candle, hemp or cotton thread, glue, scissors, hammer, flat-iron, soldering iron, soldering tin, solder, pin, ruler, pencil and compasses.

2. Materials required: Bamboo is the principal material for making the frame of a kite. It can also be made with wooden or plastic strips or iron wire. Other materials include thin but strong paper, plastic, silk or nylon sheets, dyes, thin pieces of copper or a cut-open pop-top tin and galvanized wire of different sizes.

3. Before start making a kite, it is essential to prepare a precise design drawing for the frame and decoration of the kite. It will be best if the design drawing is of the same size as the kite to be made. (For extra large and large kites, the design drawing can be scaled down.) This will make it easier to cut the materials with precision and achieve success in the first try.

4. Making the frame of the kite: The best material for making the frame of a kite is bamboo (as it is dealt with here) because bamboo is light, strong, resilient and can be easily bent by heating. When preparing the bamboos according the measurements of the design drawing, the best part of a bamboo is that between two joints, for the joints cannot be easily bent by heating. When using a long bamboo and the joints cannot be avoided, it is necessary to file off the joints and bend the strips very carefully by heating. Only old and dry bamboos should be used. Green and wet bamboos have to be dried for a year before they can be used. Rotten bamboos should be discarded.

a) After choosing a bamboo, file off the joints and split it into strips of the desired width with a knife. The strips are then whittled to the desired thickness and smoothed off with a knife.

b) Bending the strips: As there are curves and circles in a kite, it is necessary to bend the bamboo strips over a burner. A strip is to be held by the ends with both hands over an alcohol burner or a candle, the skin side of the strip away from the burner. Patience is important in doing this. When moisture appears on the surface of the strip, it is time to bend it to the necessary curve. A bamboo strip cannot be bent before moisture comes out of it. Bending it forcibly will only break it. Even after it is bent, it will return to its original shape after cooling. It is also important not to over-heat it. Otherwise, the bamboo strip will become burned and dry and easily breakable.

c) After bending, a bamboo strip is to be split again into two equal strips with a knife for the corresponding parts of a kite frame. The knife should come down slowly with its edge constantly adjusted so that the two parts will be equal in thickness.

d) Tying the frame: The way to join two strips together is to place the two strips together and make a diagonal cut. The two strips can then be joined by the diagonal cuts and tied firmly and neatly with a cord. The two strips can also be joined with a copper or aluminum tube of the correct size. The parts of most of the composite kites are joined by metal tubes.

5. Painting the decoration: Different kites are painted with different decorations. The maker can of course create his own design.

The decorations are painted on the kite's surface either after or before the covering is pasted on the frame. Another method is to paint part of the decoration before hand and part of it afterwards.

In Weifang, Shandong Province, in the past, there were kites decorated with pleasant woodblock prints of bright colours.

6. Ironing: The paper or silk for making the covering of a kite is to be smoothed with an iron after it is painted with decoration. To facilitate the pasting, the flat-iron should not be too hot.

7. Pasting: Applying glue on the frame before pasting and stretching tight the paper or silk on it. There are makers who spray water on the paper or silk before pasting it on the frame. When the paper or silk becomes dry, it will become tightly stretched on the frame. It is importantly keep the two sunken places in the wings of a winged-kite equal in depth and tautness.

8. Assembling the kite: After the various parts of a kite is assembled, the next step is to tie the bridle to which the flier's line is attached. Tying the bridle is very important for it decides whether a kite can fly or not. The number of cords in a bridle differs with different types of kites.

Single-cord bridle: The one-cord bridle has to be adjusted upward and downward, to the left and to the right, for the kite to achieve balance. It requires some skills to tie a single-cord bridle. Kites like the eagle kite have a single-cord bridle.

Two-cord bridle: The length of the upper and lower cords of the bridle has to be adjusted for the kite to achieve balance. The two-cord bridle is used on soft-wing kites like the dragonfly and butterfly kites.

Three-cord bridle: This is an improvement of the two-cord bridle to control the lengthwise and widthwise balance of the kite. The three-cord bridle is the most ordinary bridle composed of a triangle of three cords with two balanced cords above and one cord below. The lower cord is longer than the upper cords so that the centre of the bridle is one or two centimetres higher than the centre of gravity of the kite. Kites like the swallow kite use the three-cord bridle.

Multiple-cord bridle: A bridle composed of from four to as many as 100 cords, is usually used for flying a large or extra large kite, flat kite and box kite. Since the frames of these types of kites are complicated in shape and larger in surface, they require many cords in the bridle for the different parts of the kite and for the wind to strike the surface of the kite. Each of the cords should be taut and joined at a correct angle. As the saying goes, "When the bridle is properly tied, the kite flies high."

9. Trial flying: After tying on the bridle, the kite is to be taken outdoors for a trail flight to adjust the different parts of the kite and the bridle until the kite can fly stably in the sky. After the trial flight, the kite is to be stored in a box or hung on a wall. The kite will be able to fly the next time only by tying the flier's line to the bridle.

10. Storing a kite: Kites must be properly stored. A kite with beautiful decorations can be hung on a room wall for decorative purpose. Larger kites should be stored in a well-ventilated place to prevent it from becoming mildewed, worm-eaten or crashed. Very small kites can be kept in a box with drying agent and insecticide in it. A well-stored kite can be preserved for a long time.

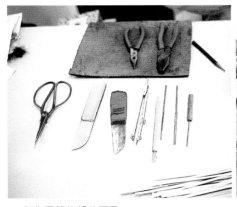

制作风筝的部分工具。
Some of the tools for making a kite.

扎制风筝首先要设计。
Laying out the design.

要按尺寸取料。
Preparing material according measurements.

取好的料要刮（锉）平。
Bamboo is filed to make it smooth.

把取好的粗料分（劈）成
若干粗细不同的条。

Split the bamboo into strips
of different thickness.

147

把取好的料按需要烤成弧和园
The strips are heated and curved.

分料，为了对称，把烤弯的料分成二或四分。
To make the kite perfectly symmetrical, a curved
bamboo is split into two or four strips.

把各种制好的条料按图纸要求扎起来。
Tying the bamboo strips according to the design.

按要求在裱糊料上绘出所需图案。
Painting decorations on the covering material.

把绘好的裱料熨平整
The covering material is
then ironed smooth.

在扎好的骨架上涂上胶(浆糊)
Applying glue on the frame.

把熨平的裱料糊在骨架上。
Pasting the covering material on the frame.

糊好的风筝凉干后，要拴提线，"提线拴得好，风筝飞得高"。
Tying on the bridle after the glue is dry. "When the bridle is properly tied, the kite flies high."

提线拴好后，拴牵引线试飞，发现问题要进行修正。
After tying the bridle, it is time to try to fly the kite and make readjustments.

把合格的风筝装盒(箱)收藏。
The properly made kite is stored in a box.

目前风筝生产主要有三种方式：一为工厂生产，是产业化生产。产品数量多，多属工艺品类的小型风筝，但种类少。二为家庭作坊，这些作坊一般为风筝世家，花样多，价格便宜，有一两种拿手风筝。三为风筝爱好者。这些人主要扎制别人没有制作的风筝，而且多有创新，精品主要出自这些人之手。他们制作的风筝主要自己放飞，或赠送亲朋好友，也出售个别风筝。

Kites are at present made in three ways: 1. Industrialized factory production, which turns out kites in large numbers but few varieties. 2. Household workshops, which are generally run by families of generations of kite makers. They produce many varieties of kites, including one or two which are their specialties, and sell them at cheaper prices. 3. Individual kite fans. Some individuals make their own kites. Many of the kites made by them are original fine works of art. They make kites for their own amusement or as a gift for a friend of relative. Rarely do they sell them.

风筝家庭作坊
A household kite workshop.

风筝工厂车间一角
In a kite factory.

附：燕风筝的扎制

燕风筝是一种硬翅风筝，它是将膀翅上下两竹条对扎起来，以区别软翅而名。中国的硬翅风筝的骨架，程式化、图案化尤为突出，燕风筝的谱式，二百多年来，至今还为人使用。

扎燕风筝的特点是："两膀对扎似半圆，上条健直下条纤；膀梢刮薄存弹力，糊成膀兜方自然。尾竹宜软不宜硬，反使竹青须去性。"

扎燕风筝是以头宽或头高作为计算膀条、胸腹和尾条的长度的。

以肥燕的骨架比例为例：

头高与头宽相同，头宽即胸宽，胸腹高为头宽的2倍，也是膀翅的宽度，膀条的长度为头宽的7倍，尾条上端在胸腹正中处交叉绑扎，尾竹根部到下膀交接处的长度是头宽的3倍。裆线为膀条长的十分之一点二五。

瘦燕、半瘦燕、雏燕、比翼双头燕的骨架匀可按图所示的比例关系进行绑扎（图一）。

骨架绑扎好后就可先进行裱糊，凉干后，可按个人的喜好进行绘画着色。

绑扎燕风筝骨架时应注意几点：

1. 扎骨架要选好竹，按尺寸下好料，刮净，然后按图要求把头、胸腹的竹条烤弯，烤时竹皮应向上。膀条要分粗细，上膀条粗，下膀条为上膀条直径的三分之二或比例相近。尾条比下膀更软、更细，直径为下膀条的三分之二。从膀根到膀梢，其间由粗到细，逐渐用刀刮削好。具体操作时，可从膀梢处计算，上膀条从膀梢到膀根处在头宽的一倍半处，用刀向膀梢处刮削，刮细、刮薄。下膀条是从膀梢到膀根处在头宽的二倍处向梢处刮削，使其细、薄。尾条也要刮削，使其逐渐变细(图二)。

2. 胸腹条与膀条交接处要劈缝绑扎。把和上膀条绑扎处的胸腹条，用尖刀劈一小缝，穿过上膀条，把劈开的胸腹条上下处绑扎紧，再把膀条和胸腹条交接处束紧。下膀条与胸腹条绑扎处，先用刀慢慢劈开胸腹条顶端，把下膀条夹住，绑紧胸腹条开口两端，再把胸腹条和下膀条束紧(图二)。

3. 绑扎好上下膀条后，把膀条两端梢交叉状绑好。交叉时要把两端劈开，然后把两端交叉在一起绑扎紧(图三)。

4. 绑扎好膀翅后，进行拴膀线。把膀线一头拴在膀翅梢端交叉绑扎处，另一头拴绕在胸腹条中间部分，拉紧后，再拴绕在另一胸腹条中间部分，然后拉紧拴到另一膀翅梢端交叉绑扎处。膀线的长度应以膀翅的软硬和膀兜的深浅而定(图四)。

5. 最后绑扎尾条，尾条绑扎好后，要拴挡线。挡线按要求长度，一头拴在下膀条的正中间，另一头拴在一长线中间。把长线的两端拉紧拴在尾条两端。燕风筝骨架的绑扎就算完成。

6. 风筝裱糊、绘画完后，拴提线。燕风筝为三根提线，做对称状。上线两条分别拴在上膀翅和胸腹绑扎处，下线一根，要略长于上线，拴在下膀翅正中间。风筝左右偏重时，可调整上提线。

7. 为了方便收藏、保存和运输，燕风筝也可绑扎成拆装式。凡是和胸腹条相接处，都绑上苇管或有薄铜片(或易拉罐片)焊接的小管，到放飞时把绑扎好的风筝配件组合起来就可以了(图五)。

Appendix: Making a Swallow Kite

The swallow kite is a rigid-wing kite. It is different from the soft-wing kites because its wings are formed by two bow-like bamboo strips tied at the ends. The frames and decorations of Chinese rigid-wing kites have become more or less stylized. This is more so with the design of the swallow kite, which has been followed for more than 200 years.

The lengths of the wings, body and tail of the swallow are determined by the width or height of the head.

Take, for example, the frame of the fat swallow:

The head of the swallow kite is to be made the same in height and width. The width of the head is the width of the body. The height of the body and the width of the wings are twice the width of the head. The length of the wings is to be seven times the width of the head. The two strips for the tail is to be crossed and tied at the centre of the swallow's chest. The length of the tail from the tip to the lower part of the wing is three times the width of the head. The length from the lower side of the body to the crotch of the tail is 0.125 of the length of the wings.

The frames of the slim, semi-slim, young and twin swallows can be made at the same ratio as shown in the illustration (Ill.1).

After completing the frame, paper or other light material can then be pasted on it. When the glue is dry, decorations are painted on it according to one's preference.

Attention is to be paid to the following points when making the frame of a swallow kite:

1. Good bamboo is to be chosen for making the frame. After the bamboo is split, cut it to size and scrape it clean . The strips for the head and body are to be bent over a burner with the skin side of the strips away from the heat. Thicker strips are to be chosen for the upper parts of the wings. The strips for the lower parts of the wings are two-thirds in diameter of those for the upper parts. The strips for the tail are to be even softer and thinner and two-thirds in diameter of those for the lower parts of the wings. The strips for the wings should be whittled until it is gradually thinner from the base to the tip of the wing. When doing the actual whittling, the strip for the upper part of the wing is to be thinned from the place 1.5 times the width of the head from the tip, and the strip for the lower part of the wing, from the place twice the width of the head(Ill.2).

2. Inserting the wing strip into the body strip: Cut with a small knife a split into the body strip at the place where it is joined to the wing strip. Insert the wing strip into the split and tie a knot above and below the split before tying up the two strips together. Make a small split at the end of the body strip, put the strip for the lower part of the wing into the split and tie a knot above and below the wing strip before tying the two strips together (Ill.2).

3. After tying up the upper and lower strips of the wings, tie the tips of the wings together. Make a small split at the tip of each of the strips, join the upper and lower strips of the wings by the splits before tying the tips together (Ill.3).

4. Tying the wing string after tying the wing strips: Tie a string from the tip of the wing to the middle part of the body strip. After tautening it, lead and tie it to the middle part of the other side of the body and then to the other tip of the wing. The length of the string is determined by the rigidness of the wings and the depth of the depressions in the wings (Ill.4)

5. After tying on the tail strips, tie the crotch string. One end of the crotch string is to be tied to the centre of the lower wing strip, and the other, at the centre of a long string that leads from one tip of the tail to the other (Ill.5).

6. Tying the bridle: The swallow kite requires a bridle of three cords. The two upper cords are tied to the places where the wing strip join the body strips. The lower cord is to be slightly longer than the upper cords and tied to the centre of the lower wing strip. Adjust the upper cords if the kite inclines to the left or right (Ill.5).

7. To facilitate storing and transportation, the swallow kite can be made in the detachable style. Reed or copper tubes or tubes made of a pop-top tin are fitted on the body of the swallow where the other parts are to be joined to it so that the kite can be assembled before it is sent to the sky (Ill.6).

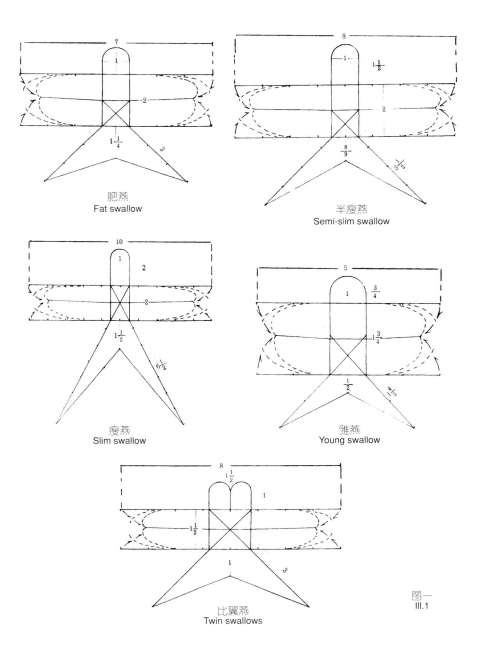

肥燕
Fat swallow

半瘦燕
Semi-slim swallow

瘦燕
Slim swallow

雏燕
Young swallow

比翼燕
Twin swallows

图一
III.1

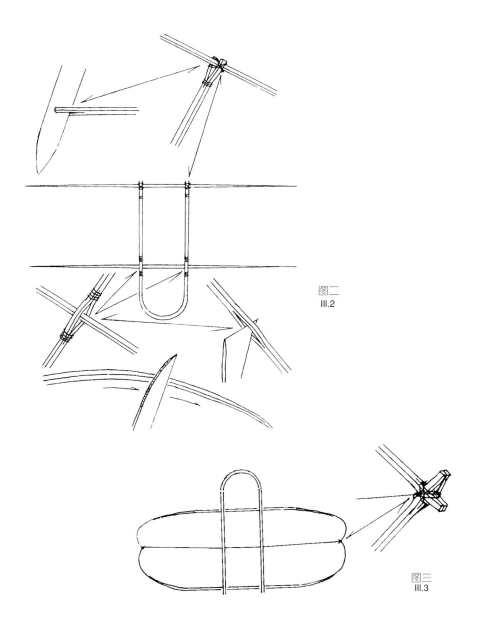

图二
III.2

图三
III.3

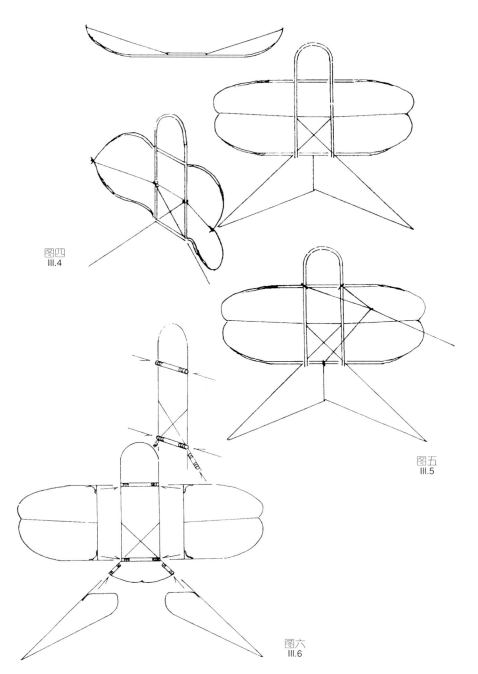

图四
III.4

图五
III.5

图六
III.6

图书在版编目 (CIP) 数据

中国风筝：汉、英对照 / 刘春根编，－北京：外文出版社，
2000.8
ISBN 7-119-02669-0

I. 中 ... II. 刘 ... III. 英语－对照读物－英、汉   IV.H319.4

中国版本图书馆 CIP 数据核字(2000)第 65515 号

编　　者：刘春根
责任编辑：刘春根
封面设计：唐少文
摄　　影：刘春根　孙树明　王文通
　　　　　曲维波　董瑞成　唐少文
设　　计：刘春根

中 国 风 筝

刘春根　编著

© 外文出版社
外文出版社出版
(中国北京百万庄大街24号)
邮政编码100037
外文出版社网页：http://www.flp.com.cn
外文出版社电子邮件地址：info @ flp.com.cn
　　　　　　　　　　　　sales @ flp.com.cn
深圳当纳利旭日印刷有限公司印刷
2001 年(32 开)第 1 版
2001 年第 1 版第 1 次印刷
ISBN 7-119-02669-0/J·1535(外)
定价：08000 元(平)